HAPPY MARDI GRAS

WRITTEN BY CORNELL P. LANDRY

ILLUSTRATED BY SEAN GAUTREAUX

Black Pot Publishing, Inc.

ISBN   978-0-9846710-1-4

10 9 8 7 6 5 4 3 2 1

Design
Sean Gautreaux www.art504.com

Published by
Black Pot Publishing, Inc.
P.O. Box 35
Gretna, Louisiana 70054

For general information or to contact the author about school readings/signings,
email blackpot70054@ymail.com

Printed in Canada

Author: Cornell P. Landry

Sean Gautreaux and I have been collaborating since he illustrated my second book, *Happy Jazzfest*. We were at the New Orleans Jazz and Heritage Festival, for the release of that book, when Sean told me his dream of illustrating a children's Mardi Gras book someday. That night, I went home and wrote the poem *Happy Mardi Gras*, which became the basis for this book. Shortly after writing the poem, Sean and I went from book signing to book signing, and at each signing people would ask "Do you have any plans to do a Mardi Gras book?". We told them that we did have plans to do one, but didn't know when it would be released. To say it got put on the back burner is an understatement. We ended up collaborating on three more books (*One Dat Two Dat are You Who Dat?*, *Monte the Lion*, and *Le Petit Bonhomme Janvier: The Little January Man*), before we had the chance to begin artwork on *Happy Mardi Gras*. This book is now the 5th book that Sean and I have worked on together. In my opinion, this is Sean's best work to date. Prior to meeting Sean, he used his impressive talent to create fabulous works of art for some of the most respected float builders in the New Orleans area. I am very proud that he has now created a fantastic piece of Mardi Gras art for me. For that reason, I am dedicating this book to him. I am proud to call him my friend. GREAT JOB, SEAN!

Illustrator: Sean Gautreaux

First, I need to thank Cornell for believing in me time and time again. I remember him pulling his notepad out of his pocket in the beverage line at Jazz Fest and showing me the script the very next day. And that is where this book began. Well, it's finally here and I have to say that I am surprised at how well it turned out.

After moving back to NOLA in 2004, I took some good advice from Arthur Hardy and worked my way into the Mardi Gras industry. I began by painting Endymion floats during crunch time, but in the end it was rewarding. One of my goals in life has always been to have 1 million people see my work. Endymion draws that size of crowd. After learning a lot from people like Joe Ory, Jordan Ivanov and Richard Valadie, I worked my way up to painting some of the finest parades in Carnival, like Krewe D'Etat and Proteus. During the 2010 post-Mardi Gras season hiatus, I answered an online post requesting an illustrator for a book. After a meeting with Cornell at his Kingfish Grill and realizing I had two weeks to illustrate his book, the challenge was on and here we are. The style goal for this book was to illustrate it just as I would if I were painting a float, with canvas, paint, brushstrokes and all.

Illustrating books has become even more rewarding in terms of personal goals. When I compare spending a week painting a float, only to have it enjoyed for three hours on a parade route, with spending time on a book that is reproduced by the thousands and enjoyed for years to come, there is a huge difference. Moreover, hearing some of the amazing feedback that we receive from kids and parents alike makes it all worthwhile. Let's keep 'em rolling, Cornell!

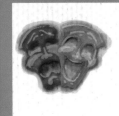

Listen my children
And you will be told
About a tradition
Of purple, green and gold

It began years ago
In the country of France
Now we take to the streets
To parade and to dance

Other cities do it
But not quite like us
You must come to New Orleans
To see what's the fuss

Carnival starts
On the Feast of Kings
Let's take a look
At what Mardi Gras brings

We take to the streets
We make no excuses
We go to parades
Named for Greek gods and muses

Flambeaus light the way
In front of the bands
Then floats make a pass
In front of grand stands

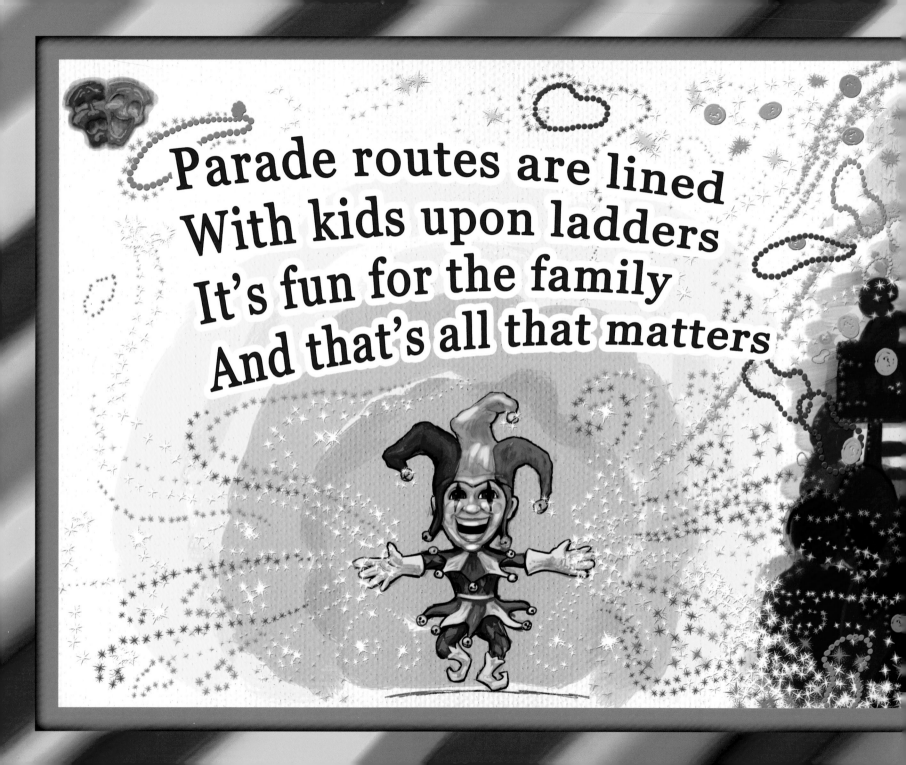

Parade routes are lined
With kids upon ladders
It's fun for the family
And that's all that matters

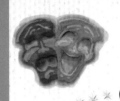

So, Mom, Dad,
Brother, and Sister
Yell to the floats
"THROW ME SOMETHING, MISTER"

Wave to King Zulu
As he passes so grand
Beg for a coconut
To be dropped in your hand

To collect them all up
Is no tiny measure
It's Mardi Gras money
They're a coveted treasure

No more balls
No more bashes
Wednesday is for Church
To mark foreheads with ashes

40 days they shall pass
It's the beginning of Spring
Now it's time to see
What the Easter Bunny brings!

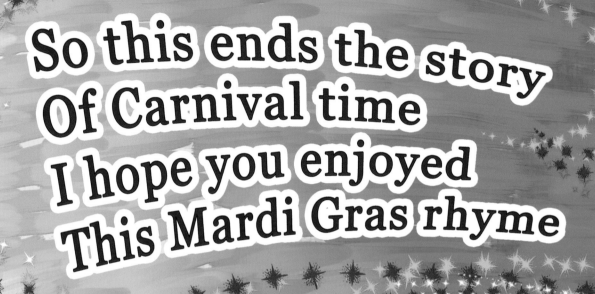

So this ends the story
Of Carnival time
I hope you enjoyed
This Mardi Gras rhyme

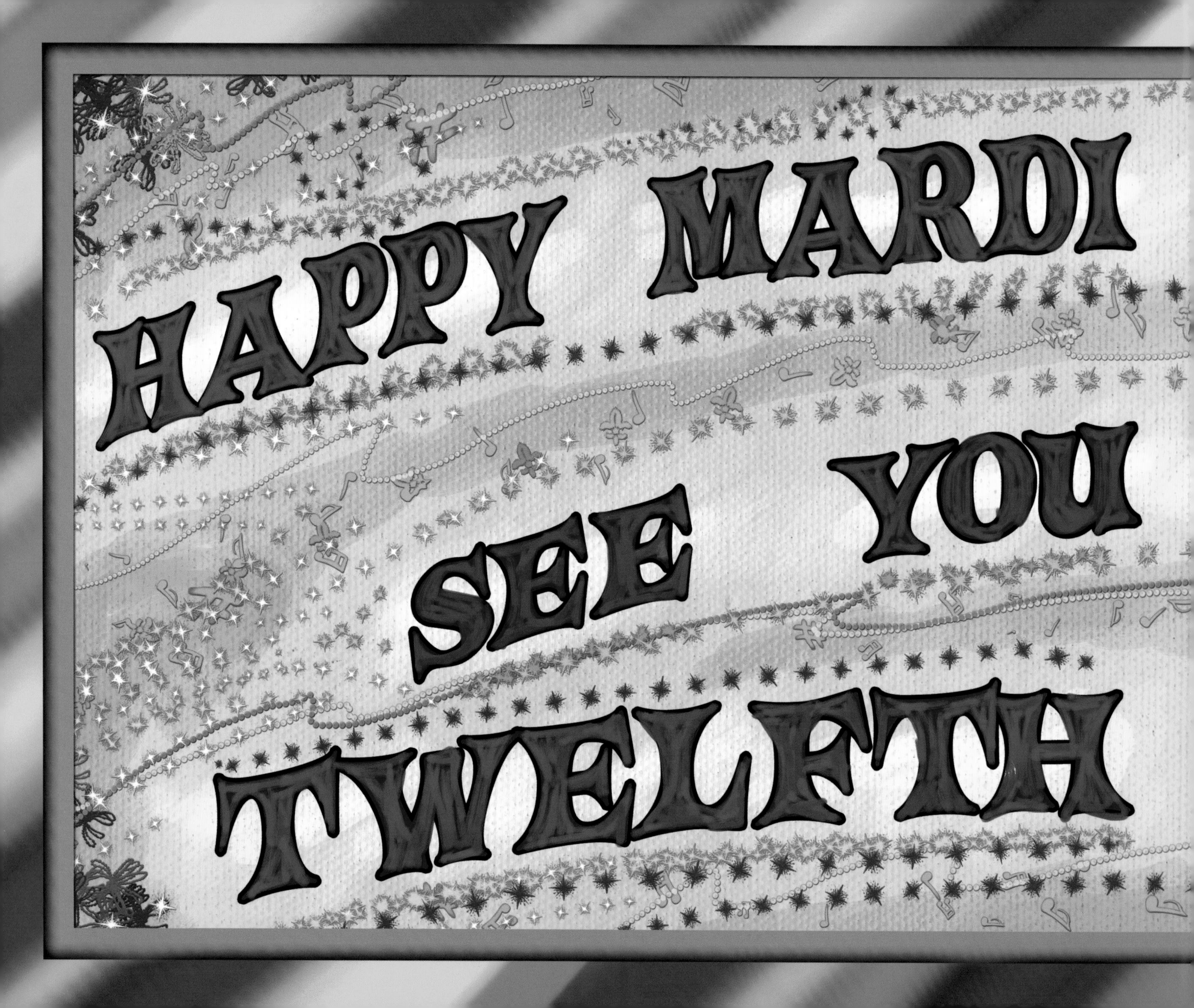
HAPPY MARDI
SEE YOU
TWELFTH

GRAS TO ALL!
ALL NEXT
NIGHT!

History of Mardi Gras in the New Orleans Area

by Rafael Monzon

Mardi Gras (Fat Tuesday) is the End of the Carnival Season which starts with Twelfth Night (King's Day - January 6th.)

1699, French Explorer Iberville named Point du Mardi Gras after a French holiday.

1700s Masked Dances (Balls) were held in New Orleans.

1857, Members of a Mobile New Year's Eve Celebrating Club called the Cowbellians came to New Orleans to organize the first Mardi Gras Celebrating club called Mystick Krewe of Comus.

Comus's Krewe (Club) helped return Mardi Gras to a Grand and Safe Celebration.

Early 1860s, Mardi Gras canceled due to the Civil War.

1870, Twelfth Night Revelers was formed.

1871, Mardi Gras King Cake was introduced by Twelfth Night Revelers using a golden bean instead of a King Cake Baby.

1872, Rex was formed to Celebrate the visit of the Russian Grand Duke Alexis. The Song "If ever I Cease to Love" was used in the Mardi Gras Celebrations, and Rex introduced Purple, Green and Gold to Mardi Gras.

1872 - 1899, Momus, Proteus, Jefferson City Buzzards, Original Illinois Club were formed.

1875, Mardi Gras canceled for political reasons.

1892, Rex gave meaning to the Mardi Gras Colors.

1909, Zulu was introduced to Mardi Gras.

1918 - 1919 Mardi Gras Was canceled due to World War I.

1920 - 1930s Mardi Gras Beads were introduced to Mardi Gras.

Med 1940s, World War II canceled Mardi Gras.

1949, Louis Armstrong was King Zulu.

Early 1950s, Korean War canceled Mardi Gras.

1960, H Alvin Sharp and Rex Introduced the modern day doubloon to Mardi Gras.

1967 Krewe of Endymion and 1969 Bacchus - the birth of New Orleans Super Krewes.

1979, Mardi Gras canceled due to Police Strike

1990s, Momus and Comus stop parading, but continues to celebrate Carnival with their Balls.

2009, Mardi Gras Floats are used to Celebrate the New Orleans Saints Superbowl Win.

Future Dates of Mardi Gras:

February 21, 2012	February 9, 2027	February 18, 2042
February 12, 2013	February 29, 2028	February 10, 2043
March 4, 2014	February 13, 2029	March 1, 2044
February 17, 2015	March 5, 2030	February 21, 2045
February 9, 2016	February 25, 2031	February 6, 2046
February 28, 2017	February 10, 2032	February 26, 2047
February 13, 2018	March 1, 2033	February 18, 2048
March 5, 2019	February 21, 2034	March 2, 2049
February 25, 2020	February 6, 2035	February 22, 2050
February 16, 2021	February 26, 2036	February 14, 2051
March 1, 2022	February 17, 2037	
February 21, 2023	March 9, 2038	
February 13, 2024	February 22, 2039	
March 4, 2025	February 14, 2040	
February 17, 2026	March 5, 2041